Joseph in Egypt

*But don't be upset. And don't be angry with yourselves because
you sold me here. God sent me ahead of you to save many lives.*
—Genesis 45:5

ZONDERKIDZ

The Beginner's Bible Joseph in Egypt

Copyright © 2013 by Zonderkidz
Illustrations © 2013 by Zonderkidz

Requests for information should be addressed to:
Zonderkidz, 3900 Sparks Drive SE, Grand Rapids, Michigan 49546

ISBN 978-0-310-74149-7

Editor: Mary Hassinger
Cover & Interior Design: Diane Mielke

Printed in China

20 /DSC/ 12 11 10 9 8 7 6 5 4 3

Jacob was a good man. He loved God and God loved him.
God blessed Jacob with twelve sons. They were all good men.

Jacob loved all of his sons. But his favorite son was Joseph.

To show Joseph that he loved him the most Jacob gave him
a very colorful robe. This made Joseph's brothers angry.

They were even angrier when Joseph told them about a dream he had. He said the dream meant the whole family would someday bow to him!

"We must do something about this," one brother said.
"Yes! We need to get rid of Joseph," said another.
And so the brothers threw Joseph into a dry well.

They planned on leaving Joseph in the well. But Joseph's brother Judah saw some traders coming.

He said, "Do not hurt our brother. Let's sell him to those traders."

So Joseph was taken far away.

The traders took Joseph to a place called Egypt. He worked hard for his boss. But one day Joseph was sent to jail.

He stayed there a long time, but God was always with him.

Joseph liked helping people. He made friends when he was in jail. He even helped one of his new friends understand a dream he had one night.

That new friend left the jail, but he remembered how Joseph had helped him. So one day, when Pharaoh had a dream, the man told Pharaoh about Joseph. The man said, "I know Joseph can help you understand your dream too."

Pharaoh let Joseph out of jail. Joseph told Pharaoh his dream was about Egypt. Joseph said, "There will be seven years with enough food. Then there will be seven years with very little food."

Pharaoh listened to Joseph.

He said, "You are wise, Joseph. Help us get ready for this. Please work for me."

Joseph worked hard for Pharaoh. He helped the people save food. And when the food did stop growing, Egypt was ready!

Joseph helped save many people.

Other countries had a hard time growing food too. Even Joseph's family back home did not have enough to eat.

So Jacob sent his sons to Egypt. He hoped they would find food in the big city.

The brothers went to see the man in charge. They did not know the man in charge was Joseph, their brother. But Joseph knew his brothers. He sold them food and sent them home.

Sometime later, the brothers returned to Egypt. They needed more food. The brothers bowed to Joseph just like in his dream.

Finally Joseph said, "I am your brother!" Now the brothers were afraid. "How could you be Joseph? You have been gone many years!" the brothers said.

"Do not be scared," said Joseph. "I forgive you. God had a job for me here in Egypt. It was part of God's plan to help his people," he explained.

"Now go back home. Get our father, Jacob, and bring him back to Egypt," Joseph told his brothers.

"Thank you, brother!" they all cheered. "God is good!"